SIMPLE DEVICES

THE WHEEL

Patricia Armentrout

The Rourke Press, Inc.
Vero Beach, Florida 32964

© 1997 The Rourke Press, Inc.

All rights reserved. No part of this book may be reproduced or utilized
in any form or by any means, electronic or mechanical including
photocopying, recording or by any information storage and retrieval
system without permission in writing from the publisher.

Patricia Armentrout specializes in nonfiction writing and has had several
book series published for primary schools. She resides in Cincinnati with
her husband and two children.

PHOTO CREDITS:
© Armentrout: Cover, pages 13, 19; © East Coast Studios: page 15;
© James P. Rowan: pages 4, 6, 18, 22; © Oscar C. Williams: pages 7, 9;
© Kim Karpeles: page 10; © Earl Kogler/Intl Stock: page 12;
© George Ancona/Intl Stock: page 16; © Frank Grant/Intl Stock: page 21

EDITORIAL SERVICES:
Penworthy Learning Systems

Library of Congress Cataloging-in-Publication Data

Armentrout, Patricia, 1960-
    The wheel / Patricia Armentrout.
        p. cm. — (Simple Devices)
    Includes index
    Summary: Text and pictures introduce the wheel, a simple device used
primarily to make it easy to move heavy loads.
    ISBN 1-57103-180-4
    1. Wheels—Juvenile literature. [1. Wheels.]
I. Title II. Series: Armentrout, Patricia, 1960- Simple Devices.
TJ181.5.A76 1997
621.8'11—dc21   97–15151
                                                           CIP
                                                           AC

Printed in the USA

TABLE OF CONTENTS

SIMPLE DEVICES

What is a **device** (deh VYS)? A device can be simple like a wheelbarrow or **complex** (KAHM pleks) like an airplane. Devices make our work easier and faster.

Early humans used simple devices to make their lives better. Modern humans still use the same simple devices. They are the lever, the pulley, the inclined plane, the wedge, the screw, and the wheel.

Wheels make travel much easier.

THE WHEEL

All simple devices have one thing in common. They give people a **mechanical advantage** (mi KAN eh kul ad VAN tij). Simple devices allow us to do more work with less effort.

Tractors use large wheels that can roll across uneven ground.

Grooved wheels keep the train moving along the track.

One of the most important simple machines is the wheel. Modern life would be impossible without the wheel.

The wheel makes it easy for us to move heavy loads. Two or more wheels connected by an **axle** (AK sul) allows us to build carts and wagons.

THE WHEEL AND AXLE

All wheels must have an axle to give us a mechanical advantage. The axle is in the center of the wheel. The wheel turns with or around the axle.

Devices like the wheelbarrow use one wheel with an axle. Other devices like a cart use two wheels connected by one long axle. Still other devices like cars and trucks use four or more wheels and two or more axles.

It is not easy to balance on one wheel.

TWO-WHEELED DEVICES

Riding a bicycle is fun. Why? You can go much faster on a bike than you can run on your own two feet. When you ride a bicycle, you are using a two-wheeled device.

A long chain connects the back wheel on a bike to the pedals. When you pedal the bike, the chain turns the wheel. The faster you pedal, the faster you go. Can you think of other two-wheeled devices?

The faster you pedal the faster you go.

FOUR-WHEELED DEVICES

You can probably name a lot of devices that use four wheels and two axles. One example is a child's wagon.

A heavy load is easier to move with a four-wheeled device.

Four-wheeled devices come in all sizes.

Even a loaded wagon is easy to push or pull on a sidewalk. It is easy because the weight of the wagon is shared by its two axles. Try pulling a wagon without the wheels. An easy job becomes hard! Without wheels, the wagon has no mechanical advantage.

THE INVISIBLE FORCE

Wheels work because they roll easily across the ground. Wheels work because they reduce **friction** (FRIK shun). Friction is the invisible force that occurs when one object rubs against another. The more friction there is, the harder it is to move.

To understand how friction works, try this experiment: Place a book or flat object on a smooth floor. Give it a push. What happens? Now put a ball or wheel on the floor. When you push it, does it go farther than the book? Which object created more friction?

Wheels reduce friction.

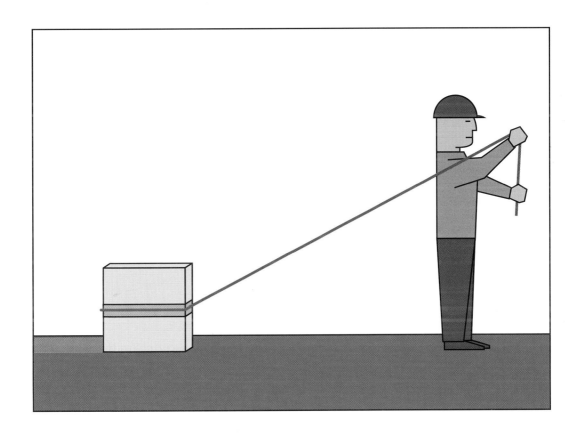

WHEELS INSIDE WHEELS

Because wheels reduce friction, they are often used inside moving parts of devices. These small ball-shaped wheels are called **ball bearings** (BAWL BAIR ingz).

Ball bearings keep moving parts from rubbing against each other. They help devices run smoothly.

Ball bearings are even used inside other wheels to keep the larger wheels turning smoothly. Bicycles, roller skates, and skateboards all use ball bearings to make your ride smoother.

Ball bearings inside wheels keep the wheels turning smoothly.

WHEELS EVERYWHERE

Wheels can be found everywhere. From the minute you walk into your house you probably benefit from the wheel. Do you open the door with a door knob? A door knob is really two wheels connected by an axle.

The paddle wheel is the moving force behind this boat.

You use a wheel when you turn on the water.

Do you have a mechanical watch or clock? They use many wheels called **gears** (GEERZ) to work. When you wash your hands, you use a wheel to turn on the water.

Take a look around your house. How many wheels can you find?

SIMPLE DEVICES WORKING TOGETHER

As you just read, wheels are everywhere. Often they don't look like wheels as you may think of them.

When wheels are combined with other simple devices, they become even more useful. Look closely at a complex device like a car. Under the hood you will see that complex devices are made up of many simple devices working together.

Very big trucks have very big wheels.

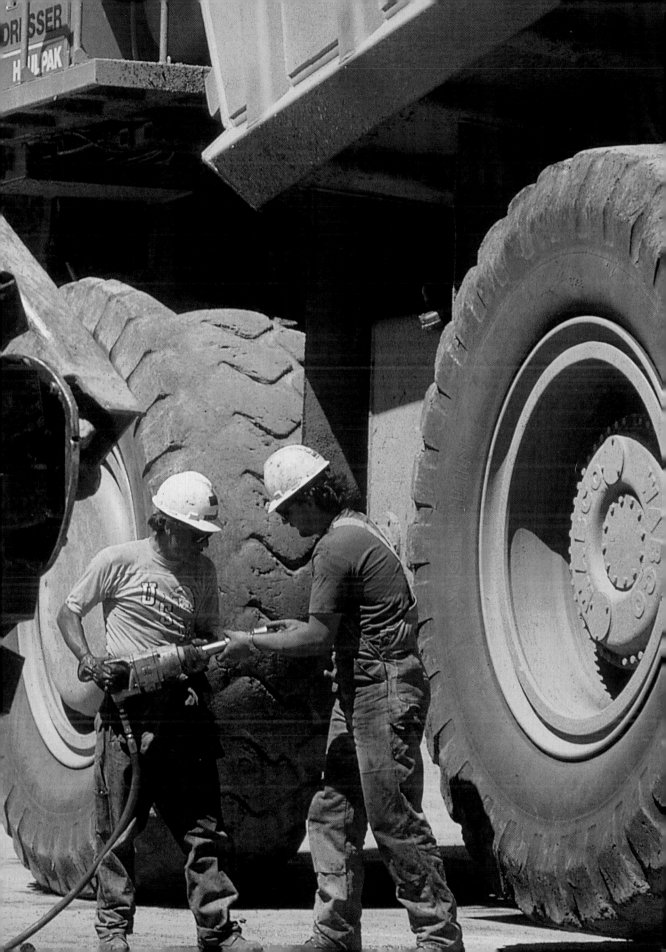

GLOSSARY

axle (AK sul) — a bar on which a wheel turns

ball bearings (BAWL BAIR ingz) — balls placed between moving parts of a device to reduce friction

complex (KAHM pleks) — made up of many parts or elements

device (deh VYS) — an object, such as a lever, pulley, or inclined plane, used to do one or more simple tasks

gears (GEERZ) — a toothed wheel that interlocks with another toothed wheel, like the ones found in watches and clocks

mechanical advantage
(mi KAN eh kul ad VAN tij) — what you gain when a device allows you to do work with less effort

The force of the water turns the water wheel at this grist mill.

INDEX